LAURENT DE BRUNHOFF

BABAR

ON
PARADISE
ISLAND

Abrams Books for Young Readers

New York

The artwork for each picture is prepared using watercolor on paper.
The text is set in 16-point Comic Sans.

Library of Congress Cataloging-in-Publication Data

Brunhoff, Laurent de, 1925–
Babar on Paradise Island / Laurent de Brunhoff.
pages cm
Summary: Babar, his family, and the Old Lady are shipwrecked on what
seems to be a deserted island, but soon they have made a new friend who
calms their fears and introduces them to his pleasant way of life.
ISBN 978-1-4197-1038-4
[1. Elephants—Fiction. 2. Shipwrecks—Fiction. 3. Castaways—Fiction. 4.
Islands—Fiction. 5. Dragons—Fiction.] I. Title.
PZ7.B82843.Baao 2014
[E]—dc23
2013020759

Illustrations copyright © 2014 Laurent de Brunhoff
Text copyright © 2014 Phyllis de Brunhoff
Book design by Chad W. Beckerman and Meagan Bennett

Printed and bound in China
10 9 8 7 6 5 4 3 2 1

Abrams Books for Young Readers are available at special discounts when
purchased in quantity for premiums and promotions as well as fundraising
or educational use. Special editions can also be created to specification.
For details, contact specialsales@abramsbooks.com or the address below.

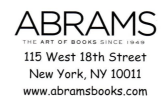

ABRAMS
THE ART OF BOOKS SINCE 1949
115 West 18th Street
New York, NY 10011
www.abramsbooks.com

Babar and Celeste, with their family
and their friend the Old Lady, left the
Celesteville Marina for a day on the water.

After several hours,
a sudden and terrible
storm carried them
far from Celesteville
and pushed their boat
onto a reef. They were
shipwrecked!

Fortunately, they were close to land, and when the storm ended, they were able to walk ashore. Flora's husband, Cory, carried the Old Lady. Flora held tight to their son, Franklin. Alexander, Pom, and Isabelle saved what they could from the boat.

They were on an island covered with vines, bushes, and palm trees that seemed uninhabited. They did not know what to do—except keep up their spirits and watch for rescuers.

One day, walking far from the coast, Babar came face-to-face with a creature that looked like a dragon. He feared it would breathe fire!

But when the dragon opened his mouth, it was merely to say, "Visitors! That's great!"

The island seemed more kindly now that Babar and his family had a friend. The dragon was a good host. He helped them get coconuts down from the palms.

He showed them where lime trees grew and taught them how to build a shelter.

Thanks to him, they had a
shower and a pool to swim
and bathe in.

Some of them even got to take rides on the dragon's back. He was surprisingly comfortable.

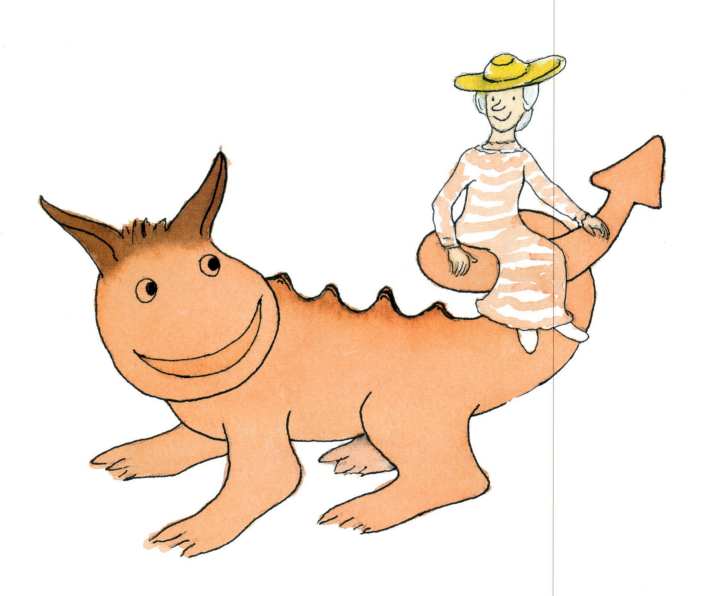

Days went by, and more creatures who lived on the island introduced themselves. The elephants had no trouble finding food and water.

At night they built a fire, sang songs, and told stories. Encouraged by the dragon, they cheered up a lot.

With eggs, lime juice, and
condensed milk saved from the
boat, the Old Lady made them
a key lime pie! But even as they
made the best of where they
were, they knew they were still
shipwrecked.

The skies near Celesteville had been filled
with planes and birds looking for Babar and
his family. The searchers were starting to despair
and decided to go farther from the city.

One day, Babar spotted a helicopter in the distance, and the pilot saw him, too! They were rescued!

They all danced for joy at the thought
of going home.

"Hurry, Dragon," said Babar. "Get your things together."

"Why?" asked the dragon.

"Don't you want to come home with us?" Babar asked in reply.

"And leave my waterfall, my coconuts, and my old friends? This is my home," said the dragon. "This is paradise."

"Of course," said Babar. "Forgive me."

So, sadly, they left their new friend behind.

But rather soon the dragon began to miss the elephants.
A heron suggested that he visit them in Celesteville.
"I will fly there and have them send a helicopter for
you," he said.

So the dragon went to Celesteville, where all the elephants paraded to welcome him.

Babar and Celeste gave him an apartment,
a motorcycle, and a season's pass to baseball
games.

It was the first of many visits. In return,
Babar's family went camping once a year
on Paradise Island. It worked out well for
everyone.